D1513585

Please renew or return items by the date shown on your receipt

www.hertsdirect.org/libraries

Renewals and   0300 123 4049
enquiries:

Textphone for hearing   0300 123 4041
or speech impaired

Read all the adventures of Jack and Annie!

1–4 The Mystery of the Tree House
1 Valley of the Dinosaurs
2 Castle of Mystery
3 Secret of the Pyramid
4 Pirates' Treasure!

5–8: The Mystery of the Magic Spell
5 Night of the Ninjas
6 Adventure on the Amazon
7 Mammoth to the Rescue
8 Moon Mission

9–12: The Mystery of the Ancient Riddles
9 Diving with Dolphins
10 A Wild West Ride
11 Lions on the Loose
12 Icy Escape!

13–16: The Mystery of the Lost Stories
13 Racing with Gladiators
14 Palace of the Dragon King
15 Voyage of the Vikings
16 Olympic Challenge!

Magic Tree House™

Racing with Gladiators

MARY POPE OSBORNE

Illustrated by Philippe Masson

RED FOX

RACING WITH GLADIATORS
A RED FOX BOOK: 978 1 862 30900 5

First published in Great Britain by Red Fox,
an imprint of Random House Children's Publishers UK
A Random House Group Company

Published in the US as *Vacation Under the Volcano* by Random House Children's
Books, a division of Random House Inc, 1998

Red Fox edition published 2009

5 7 9 10 8 6

Red Fox Books are published by Random House Children's Publishers UK,
61–63 Uxbridge Road, London W5 5SA
www.**randomhousechildrens**.co.uk
www.**randomhouse**.co.uk

Addresses for companies within The Random House Group Limited
can be found at: www.randomhouse.co.uk/offices.htm

THE RANDOM HOUSE GROUP Limited Reg. No. 954009

A CIP catalogue record for this book is available from the British Library.

The Random House Group Limited supports The Forest Stewardship
Council® (FSC®), the leading international forest-certification organisation.
Our books carrying the FSC label are printed on FSC®-certified paper.
FSC is the only forest-certification scheme supported by the leading
environmental organisations, including Greenpeace. Our
paper procurement policy can be found at
www.randomhouse.co.uk/environment

MIX
Paper from
responsible sources
FSC® C016897

Printed and bound in Great Britain by Clays Ltd, St Ives PLC

For Louis de Wolf-Stein,
who wanted me to write about Pompeii

Dear Readers,

The idea for this Magic Tree House book
was inspired by a small article I read
in the newspaper. The article said that
archaeologists had recently uncovered
the ruins of a scroll library in an ancient
Roman town. The town, Herculaneum,
was buried by a volcano almost 2,000
years ago. The same volcano destroyed
a nearby town that might sound more
familiar to you — *Pompeii*.

I have always wanted to write a book
about Pompeii, so my imagination got
to work. I moved the library over to
Pompeii and sent Jack and Annie on a
mission to find a lost scroll . . . just as the
volcano is about to erupt.

I hope you'll enjoy taking this scary
journey with them as much as I did!

All my best.

Mary Pope Osborne

Contents

1. A Secret Code 1
2. The End Is Near 10
3. Gladiators! 22
4. Scary Things 28
5. Books? Books? 36
6. The End Is *Here* 42
7. The Sky Is Falling 49
8. Nightmare at Noon 57
9. Save Us! 61
10. A Simple Explanation 66

1

A Secret Code

Jack reached into a drawer and took out his secret library card. He held the thin piece of wood and ran his finger over its shimmering letters: ML.

"Master Librarian," he whispered.

Jack couldn't believe that he and his sister, Annie, were finally Master Librarians.

He wondered if he should pack the secret card to take on holiday. His family was about to leave for a week in the mountains.

Just then Annie stuck her head into Jack's room.

"Do you want to check the woods?" she asked.

Every morning they looked in the Frog Valley woods to see if Morgan le Fay and her magic tree house had returned.

"We can't," said Jack. "We're leaving soon."

"But what if Morgan's there?" said Annie. "What if she's waiting for us?"

"Oh, OK," said Jack. "Let's look quickly."

He grabbed his rucksack. He threw in his notebook, his pencil and his secret library card. Then he followed Annie downstairs.

"We'll be back soon!" called Annie.

"Don't go far!" their dad called. "We're leaving in twenty minutes."

"Don't worry, we'll be back in *ten!*" said Annie.

OK, thought Jack. *Five minutes to the woods, and five minutes back.* Even if Morgan sent them on an adventure, they would return at exactly the same time as they left.

Jack and Annie ran out of their front door. In the bright morning sunshine, they hurried across their front garden and down the street.

"I had a nightmare last night," said Annie.

"What was it?" said Jack.

"I dreamed fires were burning," said Annie. "Everything was smoky and dark, and the ground was shaking. Do you think it was a warning?"

"No," said Jack. "Nightmares never come true."

They left the pavement and headed into the Frog Valley woods. The woods were quiet and peaceful. They walked between sunlit trees until they came to the tallest oak in the woods.

"Yes!" said Annie.

There it was – the magic tree house. And Morgan le Fay was waving from the window.

"Hail, Master Librarians,"
she said.

Jack and Annie bowed playfully.

"At your service," said Annie.

"Then come on up!" said Morgan.

They grabbed the rope ladder and
started up. When they climbed inside the
tree house, they found Morgan holding a
book and a piece of paper.

"I have an important mission for you,"
she said. "Are you ready?"

"Yes!" they both answered.

Jack's heart pounded. Ever since
Morgan had made them Master
Librarians, he had been longing for their
first mission.

"You know I collect books for

Camelot's library?" she said.

Jack and Annie nodded.

"Well, there have been many great libraries lost in history," said Morgan. "And with them, we have lost many wonderful stories."

"That's sad," said Annie.

"It is," said Morgan. "But luckily, with the help of the tree house and you two Master Librarians, some of those stories can be saved. Such as this one . . ."

Morgan showed them the piece of paper. There was strange writing on it:

Vir Fortissimus in Mundo

"Is that a secret code?" asked Jack.

Morgan smiled. "In a way," she said. "Actually, it's the title of a lost story. It's written in Latin, the language of the ancient Romans of Italy."

"Ancient Romans?" said Jack. He loved anything to do with ancient Rome.

"Yes," said Morgan. "This story was in a library in a Roman town. I need you to get it before the library becomes lost for ever."

"No problem!" said Annie.

"Do you have your secret library cards?" asked Morgan.

"Yes," said Jack.

"Good. Do not lose them. The right people will know what they mean," said Morgan. "And, as usual, here is a book to help you."

Morgan handed Jack a book called *Life in Roman Times*. The cover showed a Roman town with people wearing tunics and sandals.

"That looks great," said Jack.

7

"And take this – the name of the story I need," said Morgan. She handed the piece of paper to Jack, and he put it in his bag.

"Your research book will guide you," said Morgan. "But remember: *In your darkest hour, only the ancient story can save you. And first you must find it.*"

Jack and Annie nodded.

"Go now," Morgan said softly. "And don't forget what I've just told you."

"Thanks," said Jack. He pointed at the cover of the book on Roman times. "I wish we could go there," he said.

The wind started to blow.

"I almost forgot – I'm going to help you blend in!" Morgan shouted above the wind.

"What do you mean?" Jack shouted.

Before Morgan could answer, the tree house started to spin.

It spun faster and faster and faster.

Then everything was still.

Absolutely still.

"Oh, cool," whispered Annie. "Look at us."

2

The End Is Near

Jack opened his eyes. He pushed his glasses into place.

Morgan was gone. And so were Jack's jeans, T-shirt, trainers and rucksack.

Instead, he had on a white tunic with a belt, sandals that laced up and a leather bag.

He looked at Annie. She was dressed the same way. Morgan had made them look just like kids in an ancient Roman town.

"I suppose this is what Morgan meant," said Jack, "when she said she'd help us blend in."

"I feel like Cinderella," said Annie. "I like these clothes."

"Yes," said Jack, although he felt a little

as if he was wearing a dress.

Annie looked out of the window.

"It's pretty here," she said.

Jack looked with her. They had landed

in a grove of trees. On one side of the grove rose a gentle-looking mountain. On the other, a town sparkled in the sunlight.

"I wonder where we are," said Jack. He opened the book about Roman times. He read aloud:

"Almost 2,000 years ago, on 24 August AD 79, the seaside town of Pompeii (pom-PAY) was a typical Roman town. Many Romans went there on their holidays. They built large houses called villas and planted groves of olive trees along the slopes of a mountain called Mount Vesuvius (vuh-SOO-vee-us)."

Annie kept looking out of the window as Jack pulled out his notebook and pencil.

He wrote:

Holiday in Pompeii
24 August AD 79
Houses called villas

Jack looked out of the window again.

"It does look like a nice place to go on holiday," he said.

"We must have landed in one of the olive groves," said Annie.

"Yes, and that town must be Pompeii," said Jack.

He looked in the opposite direction. "And that mountain must be Mount Vesuvius."

Annie shivered. "That name sounds scary," she said.

"Really?" said Jack. "Not to me." He looked down at his notes.

"Hey! Did you feel that?" said Annie.

"What?" Jack looked up.

"The ground shook. I heard it rumble too," said Annie.

Jack frowned. "I think you were just dreaming again," he said.

"No, I wasn't," said Annie. "Something feels wrong about this place. I really think we should go home now."

"Are you crazy?" said Jack. "We have to find that lost story for Morgan. Besides, I've always wanted to see a Roman town."

He threw his notebook and the Roman book into his leather bag. Then he went down the rope ladder.

"Come on!" he called when he stepped onto the ground.

14

Annie just stared down at him.

"Don't be a chicken," he said. He pushed his glasses into place. "Come on. It'll be fun."

Annie still didn't move.

What's wrong with her? Jack wondered. *Usually* I'm *the worried one.*

"Come on," he pleaded. "We can't let Morgan down."

Annie let out a big sigh. "OK, but we'd better find that story fast," she said. Finally she climbed down the rope ladder.

The sun was bright and hot as they set off between the olive trees.

With Mount Vesuvius at their backs, they headed for the town of Pompeii.

"That's strange," said Annie. "I don't hear any birds."

She was right. The grove was strangely silent.

"Don't worry about it," said Jack. "Maybe they're all at the beach. Come on, let's go over that bridge."

He led the way to a small wooden bridge that crossed a narrow stream. But when they got to the stream, they found it had dried up.

"That's really strange," said Annie.

"Don't worry," said Jack. "It just means there hasn't been much rain."

They crossed the bridge and stepped onto a busy street. It was paved with stone.

People were buying things in the open shops that lined the street. Some looked rushed and busy. Others moved slowly. Children walked with their parents. Groups of teenagers talked and laughed.

They don't seem very different from people shopping in Frog Valley, Jack thought.

Except for the clothes, of course.

"How will we ever find the ancient lost library?" said Annie, glancing around.

"I don't know," said Jack. "Just be on the lookout."

They walked past shops that had huge jars in them. When Jack looked closely, he saw that they were filled with grain, dried fruit and olives. Meat hung from the ceilings of some of the shops.

They passed a noisy tavern where people were eating and drinking. A young man played a stringed instrument.

"See, there's nothing to worry about," said Jack. "This place isn't all that different from our time."

"It's not that," said Annie with a worried look.

"See, there's a barbershop and a shoe shop," said Jack, pointing.

A boy was getting his hair cut by the barber. A girl was trying on a new pair of sandals with her mother.

"It is kind of like home," Annie agreed.

They kept walking, until they passed a

bakery filled with freshly baked flat breads.

"That bread is like pizza," said Annie, smiling.

"Yes," said Jack.

The good smells from the bakery made him feel even more at home. Jack looked at Annie. She was still smiling as they walked on.

Soon they came to a large square filled with people, carts and horses, and more shopping stalls.

"Honey cakes! Stuffed dates! Peacock eggs!" sellers called.

Farmers were selling grapes, garlic and onions. Fishermen were selling all kinds of fish. A few people stood on boxes, giving speeches to small crowds.

"Hey, I bet this is the forum!" said Jack. He reached into his bag for his book. He flipped through it until he found a picture of the square. He read:

The centre of a Roman town was called a forum. The forum was the main place where people met to sell goods and discuss politics.

"I was right!" said Jack. He pulled out his notebook. He wrote:

Forum = centre of town

"Jack," whispered Annie. "Jack!" She tugged on his tunic. "Look."

Jack glanced up. Annie nodded towards an old woman who was staring straight at them.

She wore a black cloak. Her grey hair was tangled and wild. She seemed to be missing her teeth.

The woman pointed a bony finger at

Jack and Annie.

"The end is near!" she said in a raspy voice. "Go home, strangers!"

"Oh, no," said Annie.

"We'd better get away from her," said Jack, "before people wonder who we are."

He put away his notebook. Then he and Annie hurried away. The old woman cackled behind them.

3
Gladiators!

Jack and Annie hid behind a fruit stall. They waited for a moment, then peeped round the corner.

"I can't see her," said Jack.

"Who was she?" asked Annie.

"I don't know. But she looked crazy to me," said Jack.

"What does the book say about her?" said Annie.

"She won't be in there," said Jack.

"Just look," said Annie.

Jack sighed and pulled out the book again. To his surprise he found a picture of the old woman. He read aloud:

"In Roman times, there were people who could see into the future and warn others about what they saw. These people were called soothsayers."

"See? She wasn't crazy," said Annie. "She was giving us a warning. Just like my nightmare."

"Don't pay attention to that stuff," said Jack. "Soothsayers are from olden times.

People from our time don't believe in them."

"Well, I do," said Annie. "I'm *sure* something bad is about to happen."

Jack sighed. "Come on, we have to keep going. We have to find the lost library. Then we'll leave at once."

"We'd better," said Annie.

They left the fruit stall and kept walking through the forum. Soon they came to a large building. Crowds were streaming in and out of it.

"Is *that* a library?" said Annie.

"Let's look," said Jack. He looked in the Roman book. He found a picture of the building and read aloud:

"*Most people in Pompeii did not have a bathtub at home, so they went daily to the Public Baths. Not only did people wash at* the baths, but they also swam, played sports and met up with with their friends."

"That sounds like going to the pool," said Annie. "But it's not a library. Let's keep walking."

They kept walking, until soon they came to a fancy building with large columns.

"Is *that* a library?" said Annie. Jack found a picture of the building and read aloud:

"*The people of Pompeii believed that many gods and goddesses ruled the world. This is the Temple of Jupiter, their chief god. In this temple, they prayed to Jupiter and offered him gifts. Today, we call the stories about Jupiter and other gods and goddesses 'myths'.*"

"My teacher read myths to us," said
Jack. "I remember stories about Hercules
and Apollo."

"Yes, my teacher read them too," said
Annie. "I like the stories about Venus and
Medusa."

"Hey, maybe the story we're looking
for is a myth," said Jack.

"Yes," said Annie. "Come on, hurry.
Let's keep looking."

They left the forum and turned onto a wide street. Jack gasped. In front of them was an incredible sight.

Tall warriors with *huge* muscles were walking in a line. They wore fancy helmets and carried heavy shields.

Soldiers, thought Jack.

Then he saw that the warriors' feet were chained together, and guards walked with them.

"*Gladiators!*" he whispered.

4
Scary Things

Jack pulled out his book and found a
picture of the strong men. He read aloud:

*"Gladiators were slaves or criminals who
fought in the amphitheatre (AM-fi-thee-et-
ter). They were forced to fight each other or
wild animals like lions or bears. The people
of Pompeii thought a gladiator fight was
great fun."*

"That's not fun!" said Annie. "No
wonder I think it's strange here."

"No kidding," said Jack. "That's not like our time at all."

Jack and Annie watched as the guards led the gladiators away. They went towards a building that looked like an outdoor stadium.

"That must be the amphitheatre," said Jack. "Let's see what it's like."

"Oh, all right, but it's not a library," said Annie.

He and Annie started up the street towards the amphitheatre. A large crowd had gathered near the entrance. Men and women cheered as the gladiators marched inside.

Jack and Annie started to follow them, but a guard held up his spear.

"No children allowed," he said stiffly. "Run along now."

"Yes, run along! Run for your lives!"

came a raspy, hissing voice.

Jack and Annie whirled round. It was the soothsayer. She was waving her bony finger at them.

"Oh, no! Her again!" said Jack. "Let's get away from here." He started to walk away.

"Wait!" said Annie. "I want to talk to her!"

"Are you crazy?" said Jack.

But before he could stop her, Annie ran up to the soothsayer.

Jack watched from a distance as the woman talked to Annie.

"Jack, come here! Quick!" called Annie.

"Oh, no," said Jack. He sighed and went over to Annie and the soothsayer.

"Tell him," said Annie.

The woman fixed her gaze on Jack.

"All the streams of Pompeii have dried up," she said.

"Remember the stream near the olive grove?" said Annie.

"So what?" said Jack. "Maybe they just need rain."

"No," said Annie. "There're more scary things. Tell him."

"All the birds have flown away," the soothsayer said.

Jack just stared at her.

"She said that all the rats left too," said Annie. "And the cows are making strange noises!"

"But why?" said Jack.

"The sea is boiling hot," the old woman said. "And the ground shakes and speaks."

"See, I told you!" Annie said to Jack.

"But why are these things happening?" Jack asked the soothsayer.

"Because the end is near," she whispered hoarsely.

"We have to leave now!" said Annie.

"But what about the library?" said Jack.

"What library?" the soothsayer asked.

"Show her the story title, Jack," said Annie.

Jack took the piece of paper from his bag. He showed the Latin writing to the soothsayer. "A book with this title is in a library in this town," he said.

"So?" the old woman said.

"So we have to save it!" said Annie. She pulled out her secret library card.

The soothsayer stared for a moment at the card and the shimmering letters on it. Then she smiled warmly at Jack and Annie.

"Yes, I understand now," she said. "The only library I know is in the house of Brutus." She pointed to a large villa at the end of the street. "Look there. Quickly."

"Will Brutus mind?" said Jack.

"Brutus and his household are all in Rome," the soothsayer said. "That is merely their holiday villa."

"But we can't just go in and take something of theirs," said Jack.

The old woman shook her head sadly. "After today, there will be *nothing* left in Pompeii," she said. "Nothing at all."

Jack felt a chill go down his spine.

"Go and get what you came here for," said the soothsayer. "Then leave at once."

"Thanks!" said Jack. He grabbed Annie's hand. "Come on!"

"Thanks!" Annie called to the old woman. "You should leave too!" she added.

Then Annie and Jack started running towards the holiday villa. They ran as fast as they could.

5
Books? Books?

Jack and Annie ran up to the front entrance of the villa. Jack pushed the door open.

"Go in. Hurry," said Annie.

They slipped into the main hall.

"Hello!" Annie called.

There was no answer. The place seemed empty.

The main hall had a large opening in the ceiling. Below it was a small stone pool filled with water. Jack looked at it carefully.

"Oh, I bet rain comes through the hole," he said. "Then it lands in that pool so they can use it for their water."

He started to take out his notebook to make a note.

"There's no time, Jack!" said Annie. "We have to look in all the rooms for books!"

"OK, OK, calm down," said Jack. He put away his notebook and followed Annie.

"Books? Books?" she said, peeping into a room off the hall. She moved to the next room. "Books? Books?" Then she moved on to the next.

Jack trailed behind her. Even though she had already checked the rooms, he took a quick look in each of them. He wanted to see what a house in Roman times looked like. He'd write notes later.

The first two rooms had wooden beds. The walls had pictures painted on them. The floors were covered with tiny pieces of coloured stone.

The third room had a low table with silver dishes on it. Three sloping couches were placed around the table. The couches were covered with pillows.

"This must be the dining room," said Jack. "People from Roman times lay down on couches while they ate. Did you know that?"

He looked around for Annie. Where was she?

"Jack! Come here!" Annie called.

Jack followed her voice. She was in a garden off the dining room. It had a stone patio, palm trees and grape vines. In the middle was a pond with a mermaid fountain. Goldfish swam in the water.

"Look, there's another room!" said Annie. She moved to the door of a room off the garden.

She opened the door and peeped inside.

Jack looked with her. Along the walls of the room were long shelves with rolls of paper on them.

"Oh, no!" said Annie. "No books." She closed the door. "No books in this *whole* villa. Let's get out of here."

"Just a minute," said Jack. "I have an idea."

He pulled out his book on Roman times. He found a section called WRITING. He read:

Romans used pens made of small reeds. Their ink came partly from the black ink of octopuses. They wrote their "books" on scrolls of papyrus (puh-PI-rus) paper.

"Aha!" said Jack. "That's a library of scrolls! I bet our ancient lost story is in there!"

6

The End Is *Here*

Jack threw open the door to the room of
scrolls. He and Annie rushed in and ran
over to the shelves.

Jack pulled out the piece of paper with
the Latin title on it:

Vir Fortissimus in Mundo

"OK," he said. "We have to find the
scroll with this title."

They began frantically unrolling
scrolls one by one. They were all

handwritten in Latin.

"Here it is!" said Annie.

She held up a scroll. The words at the top matched the words on their paper.

"Yes!" said Jack. "I wish I could read

Latin so we could find out what the story is."

"Don't think about it now!" said Annie. "Let's go!"

She handed the scroll to Jack, then started out of the room.

"Come on," she said. "Bring it!"

"I just want to check and see what the story's about," said Jack.

He put the scroll in the leather bag. Then he flipped through the book on Roman times, looking for a picture of the ancient scroll. In the middle of the book, he found a picture of a volcano erupting over a town.

Under the picture was written:

For 800 years, Mount Vesuvius was a peaceful mountain, rising above the town of Pompeii. Then, at midday on 24 August

AD 79, it erupted into a deadly volcano.

"Oh, *no*," whispered Jack. "24 August AD 79 – that's *today*! What time is it?" He looked around wildly. "Annie!"

She was gone again.

"Annie!"

Jack grabbed the leather bag. Then, clutching the book, he tore out of the scroll room.

"*Annie!*" he cried.

"What?" Annie appeared at the door to the dining room.

"V–v–volcano!" stuttered Jack.

"*What?*" said Annie.

"It's – it's coming – a volcano – at midday!" said Jack.

Annie gasped.

"What time is it?" cried Jack.

"So *that's* what the soothsayer meant!"

Annie said. "The end *is* near."

"What time is it?" Jack asked again. He looked around the garden.

He saw something near the mermaid fountain.

"A sundial!" he said. "That's how the Romans told time!"

Jack and Annie raced to the sundial.

"What time does it say?" said Annie.

"I don't know," said Jack.

His hands shook as he turned the pages of the book. He stopped on a picture of a sundial. It showed examples of different times. Jack looked back and forth from the page to the real sundial in the garden.

"Here!" he said. He had found the one that matched. He read the writing under the picture:

The shadow on the sundial can hardly be seen at midday.

"Oh, no," he whispered. He looked at Annie. "The end isn't near; the end is *here*." Just then he heard a terrible blast. It was the loudest sound he had ever heard.

7

The Sky Is Falling

The next thing Jack knew, he was lying on the stone patio. The patio stones were trembling. A rumbling sound came from the ground.

Jack raised his head. Annie was on the ground too.

"You OK?" said Annie.

Jack nodded.

Everything was shaking and crashing down around them – pots, plants, the mermaid fountain. Water from the goldfish pond sloshed onto the patio and Jack and Annie.

They both jumped up just as roof tiles began falling into the garden.

"We better get inside!" said Jack.

He grabbed his leather bag. Then he and Annie stumbled into the scroll library.

Giant cracks split the stone floor as Jack and Annie ran to a window and looked out.

Glowing rocks were bursting through the sky above Mount Vesuvius. The whole top of the mountain had blown off.

"What's happening?" said Annie.

"I'll check . . ." said Jack. He pulled out the Roman book. He read aloud from the section about the volcano:

"*When a volcano erupts, hot melted rock called 'magma' is pushed to the surface of the*

earth. Once it gets outside the volcano, it's called 'lava'."

"Lava! That's like burning mud!" said Jack.

"It covers everything!" cried Annie.

Jack kept reading:

"There was no running lava from Mount Vesuvius. The magma from the volcano cooled so fast that it froze into small greyish white rocks called pumice (PUM-iss). A pumice rock is very light and has holes like a sponge."

"That doesn't sound *too* bad," said Annie.

"Wait, there's more," Jack told her. He read on:

"A great cloud of pumice, ash and burning rock shot miles into the air. When it rained

down on Pompeii, it completely buried the town."

"Oh, no," said Jack. "This is a major disaster!"

"It's getting dark," said Annie.

Jack looked out again. A thick black cloud was spreading over the earth like an umbrella. The sun vanished as the sky turned smoky grey.

"That must be the cloud of pumice and ash!" said Jack.

Just then the ground trembled again. Chunks of plaster from the ceiling fell on the scrolls.

"We have to get out of here!" said Annie.

They ran from the scroll library into the garden. Ash and pumice began to fall.

"We have to cover our heads!" said Jack.

They hurried from the garden into the
dining room.

"Look! Pillows!" said Annie. "Let's put
them on our heads!"

They hurried to the couches beside the
table and each grabbed a pillow.

"Tie it around your head with your belt!" said Jack.

They both pulled off the belts from around their tunics. Then they tied on the pillows like giant hats.

A chunk of ceiling crashed down near them.

"Let's get out of here!" said Jack.

They stepped over pieces of fallen roof tiles and ran into the main hall. They pushed open the front door.

A blast of heat and dust nearly knocked them over. And when they stepped outside, pumice rained down onto their pillow hats.

"Run!" cried Annie.

They ran from the holiday villa into the dark, burning streets.

8

Nightmare at Noon

In the distance, fire burst from
Mount Vesuvius. Burning rocks
and fiery ash fell from the sky.
The hot, dusty air smelled
like rotten eggs as Jack and
Annie rushed down the street.

In the forum, everyone – shoppers, soldiers, gladiators, fruit sellers – was running in every direction.

Stalls had collapsed. Carts were sliding. Jack froze. He didn't know where to go.

"That way!" shouted Annie.

Jack followed her as they ran past the Temple of Jupiter. Its mighty columns had fallen, and its walls were crumbling.

They ran past the Public Baths just as its roof caved in.

"Which way now?" shouted Annie.

"The tree house is in the olive grove!" Jack said as they kept running.

"The olive grove and the bridge ware near the street with all those open shops!" said Annie. "Remember the bridge?"

Jack looked up at the erupting mountain. A red-hot cloud billowed over it. Fires burned on its slopes.

"Head in the direction of Mount Vesuvius!" he said. "It was behind us as we came into Pompeii."

"OK!" cried Annie.

So while others ran *away* from Mount Vesuvius, Jack and Annie ran *towards* it.

On the street with the open shops, baskets and broken jars rolled over the cracked stones.

Jack and Annie ran past the bakery and the shoe shop. They ran past the butcher's and barbershop. All the shops were empty. Their owners had fled.

The closer they got to the volcano, the more the ground trembled and the darker and dustier it got.

"This is just like my nightmare!" cried Annie.

Jack choked on the rotten fumes. His eyes watered.

"Look! The olive grove!" Annie shouted.

"The tree house is just over there! Come on!"

Jack could hardly see, but he followed Annie. They left the street and ran to the dried-up stream near the olive grove.

"Where's the bridge?" cried Annie.

They looked around wildly. *The bridge had vanished.*

9

Save Us!

"The bridge must have caved in!" cried Annie.

They stared at the dried-up stream. Pumice had piled up in huge drifts, like snow.

"We'll have to get through that stuff to get across!" said Jack.

He and Annie slid down the bank onto the piles of pumice. As they started to move across it, more and more fell.

Jack tried to move through the millions of warm, greyish-white pebbles. But he was trapped.

"I'm stuck!" cried Annie.

"Me too!" said Jack.

"Remember what Morgan said!" said Annie.

At the moment, Jack couldn't remember anything. He was too tired and dazed.

"'In your darkest hour, only the ancient story can save you!'" cried Annie. "Where's your bag?"

Jack lifted his bag into the air, above the sea of pumice. Annie grabbed it and pulled out the ancient scroll. She held it up to the dark sky.

"*Save us, story!*" she shouted.

Jack felt himself sink deeper and deeper into the pumice. Suddenly he heard a deep voice say, "Rise, son!"

Then someone lifted Jack up into the air.

A great flash of fire lit the dusty darkness. In the red light, Jack saw the biggest, strongest man he'd ever seen in his life. The man looked like a gladiator — but even bigger than the ones they had seen earlier.

He held Jack with one hand and Annie with the other. He placed them both on the other bank of the stream.

"Run!" the giant gladiator boomed. "Before it's too late!"

Jack and Annie didn't stop to ask any questions. Together, they charged through the olive grove.

They jumped over fallen branches. They leaped over great cracks in the earth. Finally they came to the tree with the magic tree house.

Hey grabbed the rope ladder and scrambled up to the tree house.

"Where's the Frog Valley book?" Jack shouted. He was too blinded by ash and dust to find the book that always took them home.

"I've got it!" cried Annie. "I wish we could go there!"

Jack felt the tree house start to spin.

It spun faster and faster and faster.

Then everything was still.

Absolutely, wonderfully, peacefully still.

10

A Simple Explanation

Jack didn't move. He had never been so tired in all his life.

"Breathe," said Annie.

Jack gulped in cool, clean air. He opened his eyes. He couldn't see a thing.

"Take off your glasses," said Annie. "They're filthy."

Jack took off his glasses. The first thing he saw was his rucksack. The white tunics and lace-up sandals were gone. So were their pillow hats and the leather bag.

Jack let out a long, deep breath. As he cleaned his glasses on his shirt, a voice came from behind him. "I'm *very* glad to see you safe and sound."

Morgan le Fay stood in the corner of the tree house. She looked as lovely and mysterious as ever.

"Happy to be home?" she asked.

Jack nodded. The sound of the erupting volcano still echoed in his ears.

"It — it was pretty scary," he said in a hoarse voice.

"I know. But you were truly brave,"

said Morgan. "You witnessed a famous event in history. Nowadays, scientists study the remains of Pompeii to find out more about Roman times."

"I feel bad for all those people," said Annie.

"Yes," said Morgan. "But most of the people of Pompeii *did* escape. The city wasn't completely buried by ash until the next day."

"We were almost trapped," said Annie. "But we asked the ancient story to save us. Then a huge gladiator helped us."

Jack reached into his bag. He breathed a sigh of relief. The scroll was still there! He took it out. It was covered with dust and ashes.

"Here's the story," said Jack.

He handed it to Morgan.

"I am deeply grateful," she said softly.

"You risked everything to bring this to me. I can never thank you enough."

"Don't worry about it," said Jack. He didn't want Morgan to know how scared he had been.

"Yes, no problem," said Annie.

Morgan smiled. "You are amazing Master Librarians," she said. "Do you think you're up to rescuing another ancient story?"

"Yes!" said Annie.

"Now?" said Jack. Actually he was a little tired now.

Morgan laughed. "No. Take a nice holiday. Come back two weeks from today. Then you will take a trip to ancient China," she said.

"Ancient China? Wow," said Annie.

"Yes, wow!" said Jack.

"Go home now and rest," said Morgan.

She handed Jack his rucksack.

"Thanks," he said. "Bye."

"Bye," said Annie.

Morgan gave them a little wave. Then Annie and Jack left the tree house and headed down the rope ladder. When they reached the ground, Jack looked up.

"Morgan," he called. "What is that story about – the one we just rescued?"

"It's called *The Strongest Man in the World*," said Morgan. "It's a lost tale about Hercules."

"*Hercules?*" said Jack.

"Yes, he was one of the heroes of the Greeks and the Romans," said Morgan. "He was a son of Jupiter."

"Oh, wow. *Now* I get it," said Annie.

"I'm taking it back to Camelot's library," said Morgan. "Everyone will be so excited to read it, thanks to you." She waved to them. "Goodbye for now!"

As she waved, the wind began to whirl. The tree house began to spin. In a blur of shadow and light, Morgan and the magic tree house were gone.

Jack and Annie started walking through the woods.

"Get it? Get it?" said Annie.

"Get what?" said Jack.

"We were saved
by Hercules!" said
Annie. "We asked the
story to save us – and
Hercules appeared!"

"That's not possible," said
Jack. "It was just some gladiator
guy. The story of Hercules is
a *myth*. That means he never
really lived."

They left the woods and started up their street.

"I know it's a myth," said Annie. "But I have a simple explanation."

"What?" said Jack.

"Hercules is a myth to people in *this* time," said Annie. "But in Roman times, lots of people believed he was real. So, since we were in Roman times, he was real to us."

"I don't know-.-.-." said Jack.

"Did you ever hear the saying?" said Annie. "*When in Rome, do as the Romans do.*"

Jack laughed. "Yes." He looked up at the sky. "Thanks, Hercules," he said softly, "whatever you area."

"Jack! Annie!" their dad called from their front porch. "Time to go!"

"Oh, I forgot," said Jack.

"Yes, I hope nothing exciting happens on *our* holiday," said Annie.

"Yes," said Jack. "I hope it's really, *really* boring."

"Hurry!" their dad said.

"Coming!" they called.

Then they took off running for home – and a restful holiday.

More Facts
for You and Jack

1) Pompeii was forgotten after it was
buried in ash and pumice. In 1594, the
ruined city was discovered by workmen
who were digging a tunnel. Later, a
nearby town called Herculaneum was
also discovered. It had been buried by
boiling mud after the volcano erupted.
Many things from everyday life have
been uncovered in both Pompeii and
Herculaneum. Recently, a library of
scrolls was found.

2) The language of the ancient Romans was called Latin. Many words in the English, French and Spanish languages come from Latin. For example, *liber* means "book" and *libri* means "books" in Latin. The word "book" in Spanish is *libro* and in French is *livre*. In English we have the word "library".

3) Mount Vesuvius erupted in the year A.D. 79. The letters A.D. stand for the words *Anno Domini*. *Anno Domini* means "in the year of the Lord" in Latin, which refers to the year Jesus Christ was born – about 2,000 years ago.

4) The Romans took their name from the city of Rome, which was the capital of their empire. Rome is now the capital of the country of Italy.

5) In A.D. 79, the Romans had a powerful army. They ruled all of Western Europe, the Near East and North Africa.

6) Hercules is the Roman name for the hero from the Greek myths known as Heracles. After the Romans conquered ancient Greece, they adopted many of Greece's heroes and gods and goddesses. Heracles – who became Hercules – was one of them.

Read on for a sneak peek at Magic Tree House 14: Palace of the Dragon King.

MARY POPE OSBORNE

Magic Tree House™

PALACE of the DRAGON KING

One summer day in Frog Valley, a mysterious tree house appeared in the woods.

Eight-year-old Jack and his seven-year-old sister, Annie, climbed into the tree house. They found that it was filled with books.

Jack and Annie soon discovered that the tree house was magic. It could take them to the places in the books. All they had to do was point at a picture and wish to go there.

Along the way, they discovered that the tree house belongs to Morgan le Fay.

Morgan is a magical librarian from the time of King Arthur. She travels through time and space, gathering books.

In Magic Tree House 12, *Icy Escape!*, Jack and Annie solved the last of four ancient riddles and became Master Librarians. To help them in their future tasks, Morgan gave Jack and Annie secret library cards with the letters ML on them.

Jack and Annie's first four missions as Master Librarians are to save stories from ancient libraries. When their first adventure ended (Magic Tree House 13, *Racing with Gladiators*), Morgan asked them to return to the tree house in two weeks to go to China and save another story.

Now the two weeks are over . . .

1

The Bamboo Book

Annie peeped into Jack's room.

"Ready to go to China?" she asked.

Jack took a deep breath.

"Yes," he answered.

"Bring your secret library card," Annie said. "I have mine in my pocket."

"Yep," said Jack.

He opened his top dresser drawer and took out a thin wooden card. The letters ML on it shimmered in the light. Jack dropped the card into his rucksack. Then he threw in his notebook and a pencil.

"Let's go," said Annie.

Jack pulled on his bag and followed her.

What are we in for today? he wondered.

"Bye, Mum!" said Annie as they passed their mother in the kitchen.

"Where are you going?" she asked.

"China!" said Annie.

"Great," their mum said. She winked at them. "Have fun."

Fun? thought Jack. He was afraid that *fun* wasn't quite the right word.

"Just wish us luck," he said as he and Annie headed out the front door.

"Good luck!" their mother called.

"If only she knew we aren't pretending," Jack whispered to Annie.

"Yes," said Annie, grinning.

Outside, the sun shone brightly. Birds sang. Crickets chirped. Jack and Annie walked up their street towards the Frog

Valley woods.

"I wonder if the weather will be this nice in China," Annie said.

"I don't know. Remember, Morgan said this would be a very scary adventure," said Jack.

"They're always scary," said Annie. "But we always meet animals or people who help us."

"True," Jack said.

"I bet we meet someone *great* today," said Annie.

Jack smiled. He was starting to feel excited now instead of scared.

"Let's hurry!" he said.

They ran into the Frog Valley woods. They slipped between the tall trees until they came to a huge oak.

"Hello!" came a soft voice they knew well.

They looked up. Morgan was peering down from the magic tree house.

"Ready for your next mission as Master Librarians?" she asked.

"Yes!" said Jack and Annie.

They grabbed the rope ladder and started up.

"Are we still going to China?" asked Annie when they had climbed into the tree house.

"Indeed," said Morgan. "You're going to *ancient* China. Here is the title of the story you must find."

She held up a long, thin strip of wood. It looked like a ruler, except it had strange writing on it instead of numbers.

"Long ago, the Chinese discovered how to make paper. It was one of the world's most important discoveries," said Morgan. "But you are going to a time earlier than that, to a time when books were written on bamboo strips like this one."

"Wow," said Annie, pointing at the figures on the bamboo. "So *this* is Chinese writing?"

"Yes," said Morgan. "Just as we have letters, Chinese writing is made up of many characters. Each one stands for a different thing or idea. These characters are the title of an ancient Chinese legend. You must find the first writing of the legend before the Imperial Library is destroyed."

"Hurry, let's go," said Annie.

"Wait, we need our research book,' said Jack.

"Yes, you do," said Morgan.

From the folds of her robe, she pulled out a book. On the cover was the title

The Time of the First Emperor.

Morgan handed the book to Jack.

"This research book will *guide* you," she said. "But remember, in your darkest hour, only the old legend can *save* you."

"But we have to find it first," said Annie.

"Exactly," said Morgan.

She handed Jack the bamboo strip, and he slipped it into his bag.

Jack pushed his glasses into place, then pointed at the cover of their research book.

"I wish we could go there!" he said.

The wind started to blow.

The tree house started to spin. It spun faster and faster.

Then everything was still.

Absolutely still.

COLLECT THEM ALL!

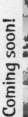